The Old Red Rocking Chair

By **Phyllis Root**

Illustrated by **John Sandford**

SCHOLASTIC INC.

New York   Toronto   London   Auckland   Sydney

For Amelia and her friend Ilana, and for Ellen and her friends Anne and Meredith. —P.R.

For Sugar Grandma Clara Tate with love from me, your daughter's mate. —J.S.

Text copyright © 1992 by Phyllis Root.
Illustrations copyright © 1992 by John Sandford.
All rights reserved. Published by Scholastic Inc., 555 Broadway, New York,
NY 10012, by arrangement with Arcade Publishing, Inc.

Printed in the U.S.A.
ISBN 0-590-60500-3

1   2   3   4   5   6   7   8   9   10   08   02   01   00   99   98   97   96   95

One spring morning Martha Jenkins put her old red rocking chair out with the garbage. She had rocked all her children in it, but the children were grown now, the chair seat was worn, and the color didn't match her new blue sofa.

3

Sam Puckett was out walking his Saint Bernard dog Fergie when he saw the rocking chair.

"Just the thing for the living room," he told Fergie. Together they dragged the chair home along with an old radio they had found.

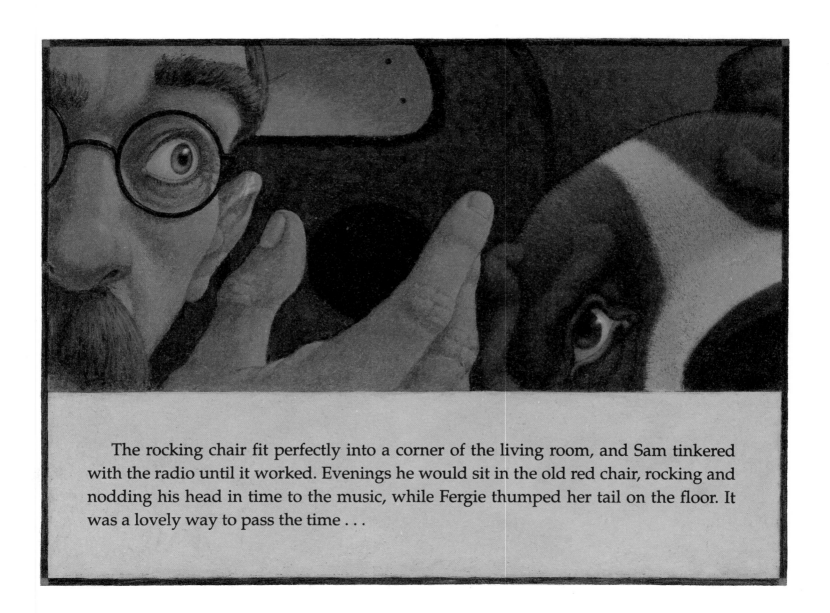

The rocking chair fit perfectly into a corner of the living room, and Sam tinkered with the radio until it worked. Evenings he would sit in the old red chair, rocking and nodding his head in time to the music, while Fergie thumped her tail on the floor. It was a lovely way to pass the time . . .

. . . until Fergie decided she wanted to be a lap dog and broke one arm off the rocking chair.

Sam was a wizard with radios, but he didn't know a hammer from a hammer-head shark. Sadly he put the rocking chair back out with the trash.

Sharifa Shannon was running to catch the bus for work when she spotted the rocking chair.

"Just the thing for my apartment!" she cried. It would go nicely with her boxes of books, her violets, and her sleeping bag. There was a scrawny cat curled up in the seat of the rocking chair, so she lugged him along home, too. She was late for work that day, but Sharifa didn't care.

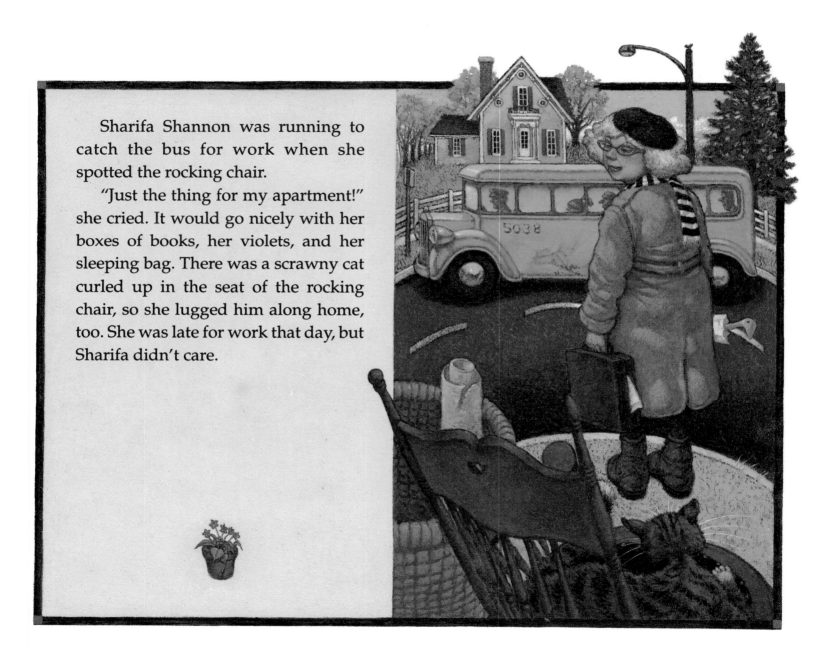

That night she bought milk for the cat and named him Allister. She borrowed a screwdriver from the landlady downstairs and took the other arm off the rocking chair. Then she and Allister sat and rocked and read together. They were cozy and comfortable all summer long . . .

. . . until Allister decided to sharpen his claws on the seat of the chair.

Sharifa was handy with a pliers and wrench, but she didn't know which end of a needle to thread. Sadly she put the rocking chair out by her garbage can.

15

The Weller twins were skate-boarding home from school when they discovered the rocking chair.

"Just the thing for our tree house," Nia told Ian, and Ian agreed. They skated the rocking chair home balanced on an old plank that they found.

The chair didn't fit in the tree house, and its back cracked when they dropped it back down. But it did make a terrific teeter-totter when they put the plank across the seat. Up and down, up and down they went. It was great fun . . .

. . . until the rockers fell off and the twins went tumbling.

The twins kept the plank to make a ladder for their tree house, but the chair they put back in the alley.

21

Agnes MacGruder was raking leaves when she spied what was left of the rocking chair.

Just the thing, she thought. She had plenty of chairs, but she needed a stool to set by the fireplace. She dragged the chair into her house along with an old blue coat that was sticking out of somebody's garbage. The coat was missing a sleeve, but the fabric would make a beautiful new seat for the stool.

Agnes sawed off the chair back to use for kindling. While a fire blazed in the fireplace, she embroidered a seat cover. There was even enough blue wool left over for a matching pair of slippers. When the legs were painted and the stool was done, Agnes sat by her fire in the mornings warming her toes. She was toasty and snug . . .

. . . until the day she slipped on the ice on her way to the grocery.

"Enough of winter!" Agnes decided. "I'm going to live on a houseboat in Florida."

She sold her house and nailed a big sign to the front porch.

Martha Jenkins saw the sign. She came to the sale and bought a teapot, two pictures, and a stool.

When she got home she made a pot of tea, hung the pictures on the wall, and sat back to admire them.

"Just the thing for my weary bones," she said with a contented sigh as she rested her feet. She sipped her tea and admired how well her sofa matched her new blue footstool.